Baby Bear
and the Big, Wide World

Illustrated by Dubravka Kolanovic
Written by Ellie Patterson

Published by Top That! Publishing plc
Tide Mill Way, Woodbridge, Suffolk, IP12 1AP, UK
www.topthatpublishing.com
Text copyright © Ellie Patterson 2013
Illustrations copyright © Dubravka Kolanovic 2013
All rights reserved
0 2 4 6 8 9 7 5 3 1
Printed and bound in China

Creative Director – Simon Couchman
Editorial Director – Daniel Graham

Illustrated by Dubravka Kolanovic
Written by Ellie Patterson

ISBN 978-1-78244-284-4

A catalogue record for this book is available from the British Library
Printed and bound in China

Inside his cosy den, Baby Bear was snug and warm in Mummy Bear's arms. Outside, the big, wide world was cold and white.

No matter how hard he tried,
Baby Bear could not sleep. He was curious.
Slipping out from Mummy Bear's arms, Baby Bear
peeped out at the big, wide world. It looked a
little frightening, but he wanted to explore.

Stepping outside, Baby Bear saw that there were footprints. Big footprints. Huge footprints! A little scared, he decided to follow them to see where they led.

The big footprints went on and on, winding down a path and through deep, dark woods. Baby Bear looked up at the sky and thought that it looked like a big, black blanket. Then he saw the moon and thought that it looked like a big hole in the big, black blanket.

Suddenly, Baby Bear began to feel very small and very alone.

Soon Baby Bear came to the ocean.
It was so big and so wide that just looking
at it made Baby Bear feel even smaller.

Baby Bear sat down and began to wish that he
hadn't left Mummy Bear's snug, warm arms.

Suddenly there was a splash, then there was a sniffle, and then a small creature flopped onto the rock beside Baby Bear.

'Who are you?' asked the small creature, looking curiously at Baby Bear.

'I'm Baby Bear,' said Baby Bear.
'Who are you?'

'I'm Sammy Seal,'
said Sammy Seal.

'Are you scared of the big, wide world too?' asked Baby Bear, realising that Sammy Seal must find it even scarier than he did because he was so small.

'Not really,' said Sammy Seal.
'In the ocean there are creatures
that are even smaller than me and
they are not scared. The big, wide world
has lots of wonderful things to explore,
but you just have to be brave.'

'I'd like to be brave,'
said Baby Bear, hopefully.

'Well, why don't you come on a big adventure with me?' Sammy Seal suggested. 'I know lots of exciting things that we can do.'

'OK!' agreed Baby Bear, feeling brave all of a sudden.

From the top of a big iceberg in the middle of the big, blue ocean, Baby Bear and Sammy Seal watched whales flipping and somersaulting out of the water and named each of the stars in the sky.

Baby Bear began to feel very brave indeed sitting on top of the big iceberg with his new friend, Sammy Seal.

Soon the big sun began to rise over the big, blue ocean. The world was filled with light and seemed like a warm and welcoming place once more. But it was time to go home.

So Baby Bear and Sammy Seal swam back to the shore.

Baby Bear thanked Sammy Seal for showing him that the big, wide world wasn't as scary as he had first thought. They agreed to meet up soon for another big adventure.

Baby Bear followed the big footprints all the way home. He crept into Mummy Bear's arms as quietly as he could and fell soundly asleep, safe in the knowledge that the big, wide world is actually not that scary when you have a friend to share it with.

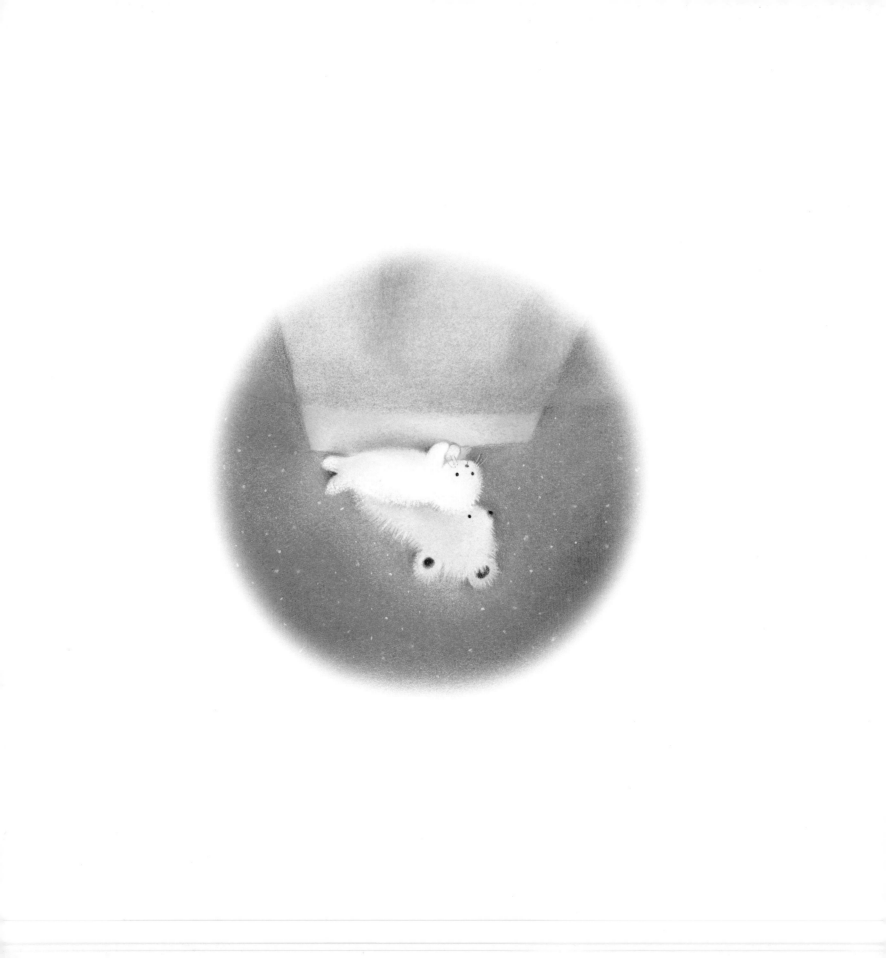

Little Penguin whizzed over to his
friends to join in with their games.
Even though he had been nervous before,
Little Penguin could not wait to come
back for more fun tomorrow!

Little Penguin shuffled closer and,
with a deep breath, slid on his
tummy and slipped easily into the water.
Just like he had practised, Little Penguin
flapped his flippers and wiggled his feet,
twirling and twisting through the water.

Little Penguin waddled to the edge
and looked down into the deep, dark water.
It looked very cold and he didn't want to go in.
But then he thought about his friends and how
they were not scared to learn new things.

Little Penguin was still worrying about
how to flap his flippers and wiggle his feet.
He could see all of his friends splashing and
sliding into the water, playing lots of fun games.

As Little Penguin got to his feet and shuffled on,
he saw a shape jumping high above him.
It was Little Whale, leaping above the waves!

'Look at this one!' cried Little Whale,
somersaulting through the air.

'Sorry, Little Penguin,' said Little Whale.
'I'm learning to jump.'

'Are you scared?' asked Little Penguin.

'Not really. So far I've only done bellyflops,
but I can almost get high enough for
big jumps,' said Little Whale,
weaving through the waves.

Little Penguin felt tired
so he sat down for a rest.
As he was sitting on the ice,
a big wave splashed him.

'Look, Little Penguin!'
cried Little Seal. 'I caught a fish!'
Little Seal whizzed off to show all of her other friends.

Waddling on, Little Penguin heard
a big splash and an excited shout.

'Are you scared?' asked Little Penguin.

'Not really. I haven't caught anything yet, but it's lots of fun!'

Little Seal saw a school of fish swimming past, so she quickly plunged back into the water.

As he was practising wiggling his feet,
Little Penguin heard a splash and Little Seal
jumped up on the ice beside him.

'I'm learning to fish!'
said Little Seal, happily.

Little Penguin continued down the icy path to the ocean. Suddenly, he saw a black shadow on the fluffy white snow. High above him in the bright blue sky was Little Bird, twirling and swooping through the air.

'I'm finally flying!' Little Bird squawked happily.

'Not really. I'm not very good yet, but I can almost get off the ground,' said Little Bird proudly.

Little Penguin was shuffling through the snow, practising flapping his flippers and wiggling his feet, when he saw Little Bird hopping towards him.

'I'm learning to fly!' said Little Bird.

'Are you scared?' asked Little Penguin.

Little Penguin was nervous about learning to swim,
but he wanted to splash and play with his friends.
So he started to slowly waddle along the icy
path towards the big, blue ocean.

It was an important day for Little Penguin.
He was going swimming for the very first time.

Little Penguin
Learns to Swim

Written by Eilidh Rose

Illustrated by Dubravka Kolanovic

Published by Top That! Publishing plc
Tide Mill Way, Woodbridge, Suffolk, IP12 1AP, UK
www.topthatpublishing.com
Illustrations copyright © Dubravka Kolanovic 2013
Text copyright © Top That! Publishing plc 2013
All rights reserved
0 2 4 6 8 9 7 5 3 1
Printed and bound in China

Creative Director – Simon Couchman
Editorial Director – Daniel Graham

Written by Eilidh Rose
Illustrated by Dubravka Kolanovic

ISBN 978-1-78244-284-4

A catalogue record for this book is available from the British Library
Printed and bound in China